WITCHLAND

A Graphic Novel By Tim Mulligan

Illustrations by Pyrink

This edition published by Highpoint Lit
For information, write to info@highpointpubs.com.
First Edition
ISBN: 979-8-9879203-9-8

Library of Congress Cataloging-in-Publication Data
Mulligan, Tim
Witchland

Summary: "This book adaptation of the critically acclaimed play Witchland is based on the author's experiences growing up in Richland Washington, 'the most toxic place in the Western Hemisphere' near the infamous Hanford Nuclear Plant. This is the story of a family who moves to this town and the unexplained terror that surrounds them. Is it owed to the nuclear plant...or something more sinister?"
—Provided by publisher.

ISBN: 979-8-9879203-9-8 (paperback)
1. Horror 2. Suspense

Library of Congress Control Number: 2024900753

Cover and Interior Design by Pyrink
Project Management by Steisha Ponczoch

Manufactured in the United States of America

Chapter ONE
Before – A Few Months Ago

Um, I think I'm a little drunk.
Shannon, you're fine.
Not much further.
That party was awesome.
You're wrecked – your fault for drinking so much fucking tequila.
You know what that does to you.
Anyways, I'm here – I got you.
Wait a minute...where are we?
Just a little detour. Trust me.
See, that wasn't so far. We're here...
You dick!
Is this the Witch's house? Why are we here?
Dammit Brett!

Come on, I've always wanted to come here with you.
And now we're here.
I double dog dare you to go up there and just tip the sticks over with your feet..
No fucking way Brett!
There's no way I'm going near those sticks!
I've heard the stories for years, and have made it a point to never come here.
Both Dana and Cindra came here and knocked the sticks over, and when they came back 15 minutes later,
there were new sticks, in the exact same weird ass formation.

Just like that.

And they say the witch never even comes outside, like ever.
No No No... I'm not doing it. No fucking way.

Come on Shannon, it will be so cool.
Just really quick. Then we haul our asses out of here.
Just tip them over...
BUT WHATEVER YOU DO...
...DON'T TAKE A STICK.

Why? What would happen if I did take a stick?

Just ask Nick. Some kid took a stick and snuck it into his backpack.
And a few days later, he got THE CANCER.

That's such bullshit Brett! It's Richland
people get THE CANCER here all the time!
We live by a nuclear power plant for Chrissakes. Nick's whole family got THE CANCER.
And Nick worked out at Hanford that summer. No way it was because of a stick in his backpack.

And besides – do you know anyone who's actually seen her?

My aunt went to school with her.
She was supposedly like totally normal in high school.
Then she went on a church mission somewhere like overseas or something, and then came back all possessed and shit, like the Exorcist.

And while she was gone, her dad like died out at Hanford, and they say her mom died of THE CANCER – leaving her all alone in this scary house, all by herself.

People have seen her like levitating in strange places, like near that church down the street
where people are always finding like shitloads of her long witchy ass gray hair in the dumpster.
Ask Darren – he mows the lawn there – and sees that shit all the time.

Anyways,
just do it – just knock them over and come back – I'll give you 20 bucks!

How much will you give me if I ring her doorbell?

Are you crazy? Don't ring her doorbell.
Just tip them over and let's go.
Or let's just call it off, and get the hell out of here.
This is freaking me out.

Whatever Brett. Here goes...

TICK

Let's go!

RRRING

Holy fuck.
Holy fuck.

Abs te longo esto.
Abs te longo esto.
Abs te longo esto.
Stulta puela.
Oh my God, I'm shaking! She was there! I think she cursed me.
Oh shit oh shit
oh shit
oh shit!
Jesus Shannon, what just happened?
Why did you go up to the door?
Are you fucking nuts?
What the hell did you do?
Is that a stick? That's a stick!
What the hell Shannon?
You were just supposed to tip them over. Are you insane?
I don't know. I freaked out!
I forgot if I was supposed to kick them over or grab one. I'm so stupid.
What do I do with it?

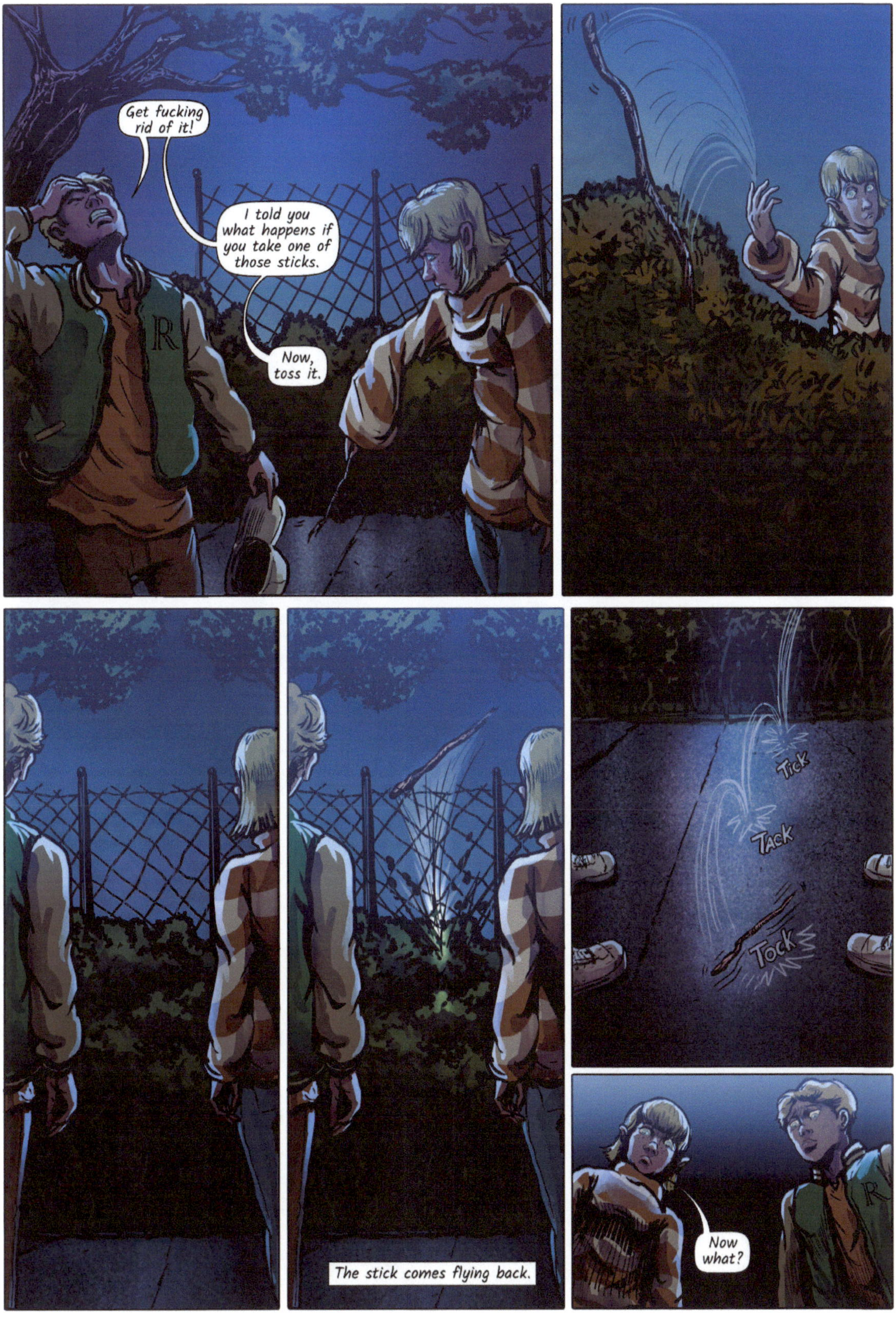

Get fucking rid of it!

I told you what happens if you take one of those sticks.

Now, toss it.

The stick comes flying back.

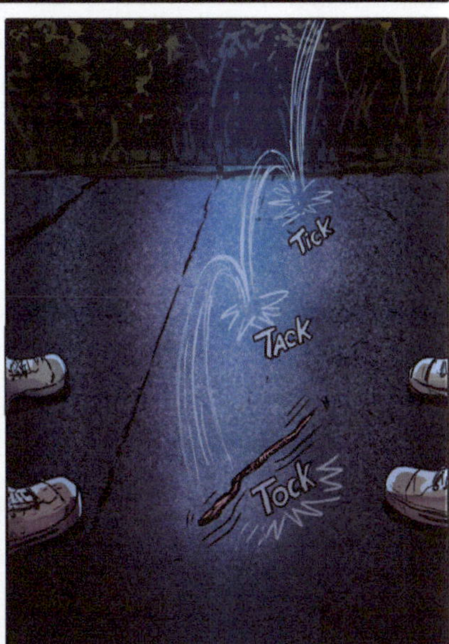

NO!
RUN SHANNON!

Chapter TWO
Before – A Few Days Ago

Seattle
...it's 12 months to the day since Seattle's Capitol Hill Neighborhood protest ended.

Many businesses remain shuttered or closed.
Though the rioting has subsided, COVID continues to rage...

Well there's my beautiful daughter. How was school?
Did you slay your Latin final?
Hey Dad.
Good. School was good. Actually, I think I crushed it.

Well, it looks like you slayed in the fashion department.

GURRL... Ali, of course you crushed it. You crush everything. You're a crusher.
I wish I could say your incredible linguistics knowledge came from me. Or your Pops.
Hell, I barely even passed a year of Spanish in high school, let alone four languages like you...

Oh, give me a break. Jesus. It's coffee. Just coffee.
It's Seattle, for God's sake. I'm a coffee drinker.

Just checking...
...Dad, it's 3:30. Have you been sitting around drinking coffee all day?

I'm closing the restaurant tonight. I need my energy.
And thanks to your watchful eye, I haven't touched booze in three months. The two of you watch me like hawks.
For good reason. You know what we all went through the last time.

I'm so proud of you. New healthy life, new job – and tonight, can you bring me home some food?
Consider this my preorder of that Truffle Oil pizza thing.
YUM.

Hi honeys, I'm home!

Well hey you. Wait – it's early – why are you home?

No biggie.
Just wrapped things up early.
Wanted to spend a little extra time with my two favorite people.

You never come home early. What's up.

Well, okay then, I guess we're doing this now.
Van – love of my life... beautiful daughter of mine... please gather around.

Okay – you know how I've been saying for a few years now that I feel like my job has hit a dead end?
That I'm not sure what is next for me?

Sweet Jesus.
Here we go.

Simmer down.
Let him speak.

Well, a few weeks ago, I was head hunted.
I got a call, about a job. And I took the bait; I took the call.
And I interviewed and today...I was given an offer.

Pops, that's amazing!
Congratulations!

You interviewed for a new job and didn't say a word to me?
To us?
Okay, surprise and slight concern aside, congrats on the offer.
But I know that look. There is another shoe about to drop here.

Okay, just listen first, before anyone freaks out.
The opportunity is incredible.
It's an Environmental Engineer job, like mine now but with triple the pay.

And...

But it's not in Seattle. It's in Eastern Washington. Richland.
You know, beautiful rolling hills, the Columbia River...

Richland? Give me a fucking break.
There's no way in hell we're moving to Richland.
Or Eastern Washington.
No way.

Just please calm down a minute and hear me out.
Like I said, this job is over triple my pay. We can buy a big house, on the river there!
We will never be able to buy a house here, we can't afford it.
Aren't you guys sick of living in a cramped apartment.

And sick of the chaos around us, the violence, the homelessness?
We need a fresh start. Fresh air. Van, this will be good for you too – a fresh start for all of us.

What about Ali? She don't need no "fresh start." She's thriving here.
You want to uproot her from the life and the school where she's obviously excelling, and swoop her off to Richland, Washington, for her senior year of high school?

Pops, I'm happy for you, and proud of you for getting such a great offer.
But I'm with Dad I. really don't want to move.
I only have one more year here. I'm President next year of our Debate Team, and Latin Club. And look at him –

Look how good he's doing now! He hasn't had a drop – of alcohol – in months,
he has a new job managing a cool restaurant – you want to take him away from all of that?

Wait a minute. What's the job exactly?
Don't tell me it's at the Hanford nuclear plant?
It's technically not a "nuclear plant." Yes, it's at the Hanford cleanup site –

Ummm...Hanford is a nuclear site, Pops. Don't sugar coat this.
It's a 2-year contract, that's it, working on the cleanup and soil testing of one small area. That's it. Two years. It's not just about me – it's for –

Pops, we know it's not safe there.
You and I together watched that whole series on King 5 News...
...and 60 Minutes...that place is dangerous – and toxic!
It's for us. We can finally make some good money – and save for Ali's college.
And the schools there are great – Ali, you can be just as active there in their clubs, activities...

Pops, you will be right in the thick of the radiation. What if you get exposed, get cancer.
You know good and well a lot of people get cancer there.
...people don't get cancer there.

Say what?

Okay,
so they may have
in the past.

Jesus...

That was years ago – the Downwinders.
They grew up there, got exposed – back in the 40's and 50's.
They quit producing that toxic plutonium stuff back in the 80's – that's all in the past!

Richland is thriving now!
Great economy, great, schools... the river! This is our chance to shake things up. Two years, I promise. Two years.
New house. How about a boat? I'll throw in a boat.

Jared, it's not just the nuclear plant I'm worried about.
You think Richlanders are going to take kindly to a gay couple with a black daughter?
We've heard the stories from our friends from there – it's not exactly a model community for diversity.
Well now I'm even more excited. Great.
Jared, maybe you go. Ali and I will stay here.
Let Ali finish her senior year in Seattle. You can come visit us on the weekends.
Ali, it would be you and I. Alivan.
V a n a l i.

Van, we can't afford to have two residences.
And I don't want to split up this family. We all go, or I turn it down.

Look. This is obviously great news for you. And a house on the river would be nice.
But I want it on record that I don't want to go.
Do I have a say in this at all?

Okay. Okay. I will turn it down.
And we will stay in this cramped apartment, and we will continue to live paycheck to paycheck. With very little to spare for college.

Well shit.
Will I be able to pick out this new river house you speak of?
Ali, you get to pick out the boat.

Yes and yes.
Look – I love you both so much. This is our chance to do something different. Change of scenery.
Let's look at this as a two-year adventure. After two years, who knows.
Ali will be in some amazing college, killing it.
And Van we can decide then what our next steps should be.
We'll take Richland by storm, like trail blazers.

Well, it sounds like the decision has already been made.
When do we have to go? Should I start packing like right now?

I have not accepted yet.
I wanted to discuss this with you both first. If I accept, yes – it's this summer. In a month.

Chapter THREE
Week One

Welcome to Hanford
WHERE SAFETY COMES FIRST

Well, that's the last box. Home sweet home.
Yikes.

Well, whatever you think of the new place – nice job team.
We did it... new house – remember this place is temporary – new town, Ali's first week in a new school –
I'm proud of my trail blazing family. Everybody good?

Can't you tell – we're glowing! And no, that's not sweat –
it's radiation.
I wonder, can it happen that quickly?
Let's keep focusing on the positive. Think about water skiing.
A quiet, crime-free existence. Ali's great new school. You are going to do great here. We all are.

Yes, I'm on board, and trying to remain positive. However, don't ask me what great things
I'm going to do in this Podunk town, and this shitty house.
What's it called again? A D house?

It's an F house.
Yeah, as in fucked up house.

Nice, Ali. Nice.
Anyways, you know this is just temporary until our new house is ready.
At least we didn't find ourselves in a B house... rumor has it they are the worst, full of bitches.

We should be there.
The Bitch House.

Why are they lettered houses again?
When the government "created" Richland – and Hanford – in the 40's, they
built these old homes for the townsfolk they brought in to work there.
They differentiated the models by letters.

I know, you wish we were in an H house – word from the 50's housewives is that those were – wait for it
–da bomb.

Dad joke.
That joke bombed.

Oh, how I long for an H house... our own whore house!
Ummm...that would be a W house. Which I don't believe exists.
And you two are like 7th grade girls.

Ohhh.
A W house of our own. Sounds so ominous. Like a ...

WITCH HOUSE!
Eeeek!

Well, we will make this cozy little Fucked Up House our own.
I can't believe I'm going to a school in a town that built atomic bombs to blow people up, and my high school mascot is an atomic bomb.
Go Bombers.
Go Bombers.

Look... let's give it our best...
make friends, contribute to Richland society.
Jared, are you sure we aren't going to get cancer?
I don't want to become a Downwinder.

Honey, we aren't getting cancer, we aren't getting radiated...
...and you know I'll be covered head to toe at work in my new fashionable state of the art HAZMAT suit. Super sexy.
If you say so, Silkwood.

Well, that would make you Cher.
Your dream come true.
Smack

♫ If I Could Turn Back Time ♪
... Jesus, I'm singing to the A is for Amityville Horror House across the street.
Didn't your relocation company do their due diligence and check out the neighborhood?
Van, this neighborhood is fine. Okay, so these government houses are old and a bit run down.
And yes, that house has definitely seen better days.
Let me guess – it's an M house...
THE MURDER HOUSE!

Wait...what is that girl doing outside?
Hey, I know her. I sit by her in like two classes.
Her name is Shannon. Do you think she's okay? She doesn't look okay.

Uh, hard no. Not okay.
I'm going out there.

Hey Shannon. I'm Ali - from school?
I sit by you in English and Chemistry.
Are you okay?

Oh hey. Yeah, hi.
I'm Shannon. What's your name?

It's Ali.
We just moved in this house a few weeks ago, from Seattle.

Ummm... do you want to come in?
Sure.

Oh good God.
Dad, Pops, this is Shannon. We go to school together.

Hi Shannon nice to meet you. I'm Van.
And this is my husband, Jared.
Nice to meet you Shannon.
Van, let's go finish unpacking in the living room.

So...do you live around here?
What?
Oh. No, I live on the other side of town.
Oh cool. What are you doing over here then?

Wait. You have two dads?

Yup, I have two dads.

But you're black.
Yes, I am black. And I have two dads.
They adopted me when I was a baby. And we just moved here a few weeks ago.

That's cool. I don't know anyone in Richland with two dads.
Or parents of a different color.
Really? God, it's so common in Seattle.
You don't have any gay friends? Black friends?

Ummm...no ...not really. I think my friend's brother is gay, but he has not ever like come out or anything.
My dad works out at the Hanford nuclear cleanup site.

You don't need to say all that cleanup stuff. Just say he works at THE AREA.

Welcome to Hanford
WHERE SAFETY COMES FIRST

All of our parents work out there.
A lot of the kids at our school work there in the summer also.
Haven't you noticed that we all glow in the dark.

That's funny.
Okay, my one dad – Pops – works out at THE AREA. My other dad doesn't work yet – he's just – like, a house husband?

Wow – you live in Richand and have two dads. I think it's cool.
But I maybe wouldn't tell others at school that. It might not go over so well. People around here aren't used to anything... different...

I can't believe you live across the street from her.

Her? Who's her? Someone from our class?
No, Judith's house. The Witch.

Wait, what?
What witch?
Right there, across the street. There's an old lady who lives there – we call her the Witch.

See – look at her sticks.
Sticks?
Yeah, look there – there's a pile of sticks on her walkway. They are always there.
No one has ever seen her put them there. But sometimes kids will mess with them – and take one, or kick them over.
And somehow they always quickly get stacked back in place.

How do you know she's a witch?

Everyone in town knows about her. She has lived there forever.
Apparently she went to some foreign country somewhere on some kind of religious pilgrimage after graduation, and came back all possessed – and touched.
You don't see her much, if ever. But every now and then you'll hear of people seeing her around town, in all like Stevie Nicks black long flowy things, and a veil over her face.
But I've seen her.

Why sticks? I don't get it.

WHATEVER YOU DO, DON'T TAKE A STICK!

There's all kinds of crazy stories of kids who took a stick, and then like died or whatever.
Or got THE CANCER. Just this past summer I was there – with my boyfriend Brett – and he made me grab a stick.

What happened?
Since then, I keep seeing weird visions. I swear I'm going crazy.
Now the whole town thinks I'm crazy. But yes, I took a stick, and she was there, and she pointed at me.
I'm pretty sure she put a curse on me. I had nightmares for weeks. I still have them, but not as much as I used to.
But you're okay now?

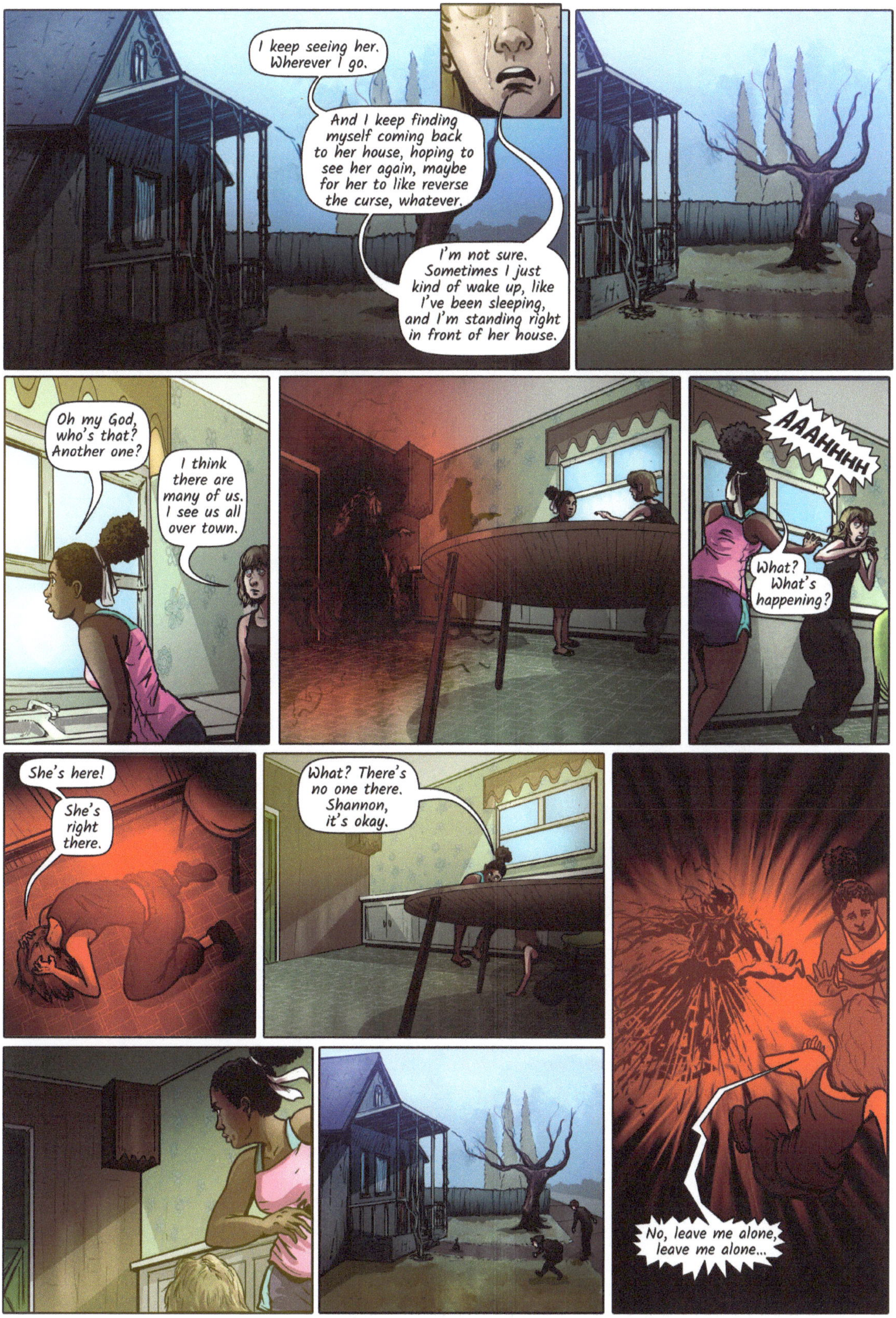

I keep seeing her. Wherever I go.
And I keep finding myself coming back to her house, hoping to see her again, maybe for her to like reverse the curse, whatever.
I'm not sure. Sometimes I just kind of wake up, like I've been sleeping, and I'm standing right in front of her house.

Oh my God, who's that? Another one?
I think there are many of us. I see us all over town.

Jesus Chris, what the hell is happening here?
Is she okay?
Shannon, it's okay. We are here with you. There is no one here but us. You're safe here.

That's so not true. I'm not safe here.
You guys aren't safe here. No one is safe here. Not here, or anywhere near her.
Or anywhere in this town.

Stulta puella.
Nunc maledictus es.
Nunc maledictus es.

Chapter FOUR
Week Three

So darling, how's the nuclear clean up going?
Did you get it all cleaned up?

Ha Ha. No, it's not all cleaned up.
I told you this is a 2-year project. But thanks for asking. My first week was -
Can we stop for a minute and talk about that?
Are we all just going to ignore the fact that Dad's drinking again?
Ali honey, Jared and I talked about it - since I'm not working currently, I'm allowing myself one glass a day - that's it!

And you're okay with this? After what happened last time?
Look, your dad went through a bad spell in Seattle, during the riots and COVID, and closure of the restaurant, and things got... out of hand.
Let's let him manage this like a functioning adult.

Thanks love. So, does your office have a good view of the reactors?
No, I don't have a view of the reactors. I look out at a gravel parking lot. But our field work is all around the reactors.
We are currently pretty much stuck in a tunnel not far away from my office. No sushi bar, no barristas, no Pelotons. You'd hate it.

So... you promise that they are not producing radioactive materials anymore.
You know they didn't even tell the poor townsfolk back in the 40's what in the hell they were doing out there. How can we know the truth...

...

...it's like the Manhattan Project. Everything is SOOOO top secret.
What exactly are you cleaning up anyways? And how can you be so sure you won't get hurt?
We all know the history of workers getting sick out there.
You seem to be downplaying that you are working at the most radioactively contaminated site in the country.

Ali, stop worrying. I won't get hurt. It's been years since anyone got hurt out there.
It's safe, I promise.

Pops, I don't think we should be here. Dad's back to drinking –
you are working out there right next to the reactors – and us - there are so many cancer stories from people living around here.

Ali, we've talked about this...
...and that's just part of it. I think I'm one of the only, if not the only, black kids at my school. And there are like no gay parents, or gay people for that matter. We stand out like sore thumbs. This place sucks.

Ali. Van. Remember what we talked about, and all agreed to. We are a team. And we are also what?

Trail Blazers.

Right. We are trail blazers here. Let's stick with the plan.
Look at the good things – it's safe, we are getting our own house... hell, we're getting a boat. We are going to live on a beautiful river.
Van, you just need to get out and get a job, get out of this house. And remember team –
Richland is known for having the best donuts in the state. Made with potatoes. Spudnuts! I'll bring some home tomorrow.

There's something else.

What else?
Come look.
See that house across the street?
A real witch lives there.
Everyone knows about her, except apparently us, since we are the damn fools who rented a house right across the street from her.
What the hell are you talking about. What witch?
I'm telling you, she's a witch. She grew up here, and somehow got possessed and turned into like a witch in some foreign country or something.
Who knows, maybe she's a downwinder, or an up-winder, or a windstormer or whatever the hell they're called. And look on her walkway and tell me what you see.

An old doormat?
No, not the doormat. What else do you see?

The sticks.
There's a little pyramid thing set up with sticks.

Oh, shit.

Exactly. Apparently no one ever sees her put the sticks there, in that weird formation. But if you kick them over, they mysteriously turn into a perfect pyramid the next time you go back. It's so creepy.
Oh – and Shannon told me if you take a stick, you are like cursed. And you might get sick, or even cancer.
I researched online – sticks are a big part of witchcraft.
These piles mean to stay away. This shit is real. And now we have to stare at them while washing dishes.

That's what Shannon was freaking out about the other day – she took a stick last summer, and has been acting batshit crazy ever since.
She thought she saw the Witch, here in our kitchen – I didn't want to tell you guys, since I knew it would freak you out – especially him...
...and I didn't want you to think my one semi-friend here in this town was crazy.

Jesus. Okay. Can we just make a family pact that we won't ever touch those damn sticks?
We are only in this house for like three more months – let's all try to hold off on that urge.

I'm going upstairs. I hate it here, Can't we just go back to Seattle?
Van, I'm heading upstairs too.
I'm going to stay here and finish up the dishes.

A few hours later...

BOO!

God dammit you bitch. You almost scared me to death!
Hahaha!

Jesus Van, what are you doing? It's after 10:00! Sneaking more wine?
I believe you already hit your one-glass ration. Come to bed.
Shhh. I think I saw something or someone out there. Outside of her house. I think she's out there.

I don't see anything. Wait, there is someone out there.

Chapter FIVE
Week Four, Wednesday

This project is never ending.
How much longer do you think we have at this place?

I'd say we should be done with this tunnel hopefully in the next few weeks.

Can you hand me your detector?
How long have you been working on this one tunnel?
Looks like you've made a lot of progress.

It's been a few years now. It seems never ending though. We're getting there...

HANFORD
Dangerous
Radioactive

What's going on? Are you okay?

There's something in my suit!
I can feel it!

Jesus, that was freaky. I swear I felt something crawling in my suit.

I think I'm good. Sorry. No idea what just happened.
Back to work...

CRACK

Holy shit! What was that?

I think it's caving – watch out!

Where's the new guy?

Attention all Hanford workers at 200 Area West.
There has been an accident at the Plutonium Extraction Facility. All employees are being asked to take cover inside, and not leave the building.
At this time, there are no reports of radiological release. But as a precaution, please take cover until given a clear signal.

Cough
Cough
Cough

Cough
Cough
Wheeezz
Cough

I can't breathe.
Cough
I can't breathe.
Cough
Cough
Cough
Cough

Chapter SIX
Week Four, Thursday

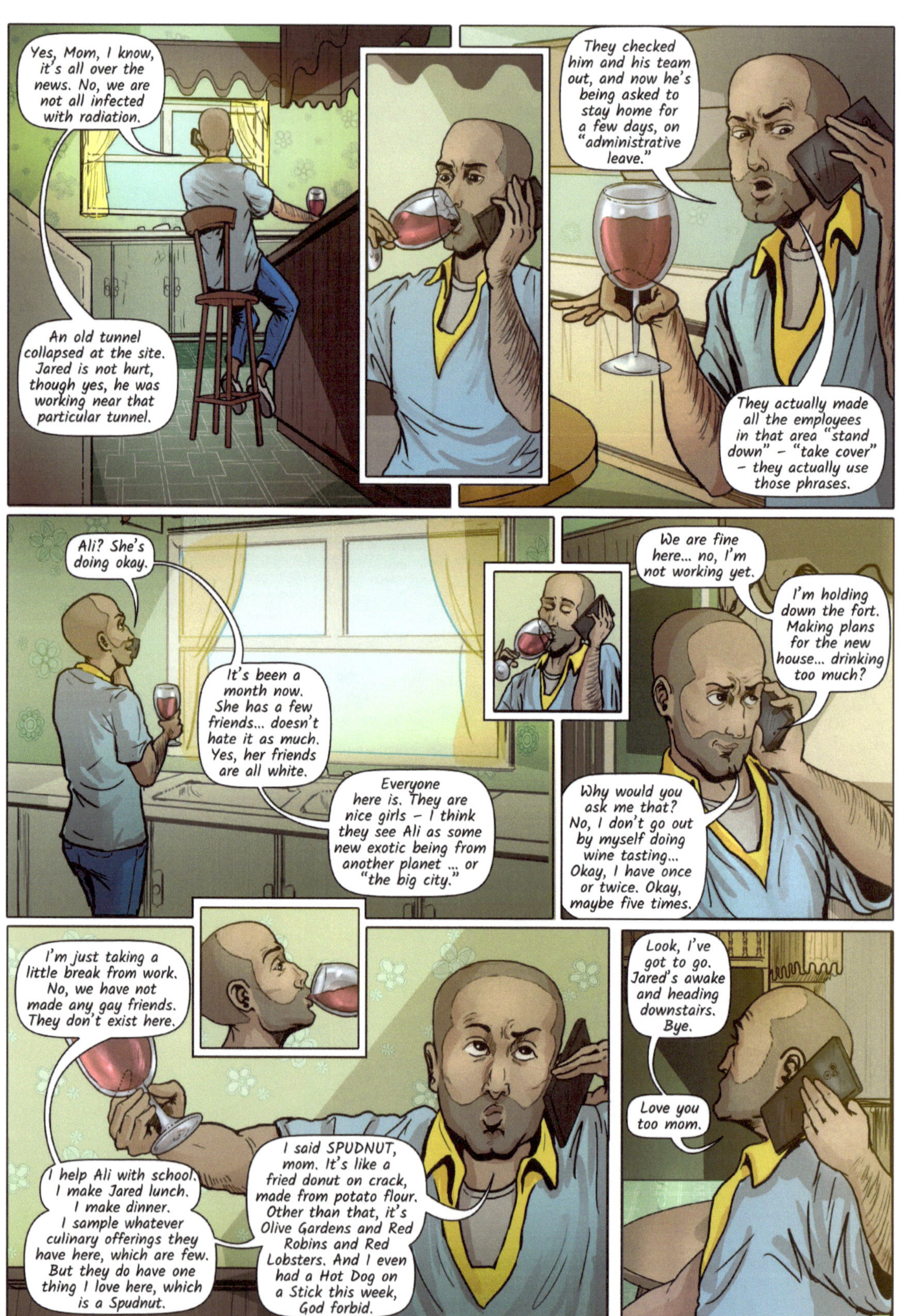
Yes, Mom, I know, it's all over the news. No, we are not all infected with radiation.
An old tunnel collapsed at the site. Jared is not hurt, though yes, he was working near that particular tunnel.
They checked him and his team out, and now he's being asked to stay home for a few days, on "administrative leave."
They actually made all the employees in that area "stand down" – "take cover" – they actually use those phrases.
Ali? She's doing okay.
It's been a month now. She has a few friends... doesn't hate it as much. Yes, her friends are all white.
Everyone here is. They are nice girls – I think they see Ali as some new exotic being from another planet ... or "the big city."
We are fine here... no, I'm not working yet.
I'm holding down the fort. Making plans for the new house... drinking too much?
Why would you ask me that? No, I don't go out by myself doing wine tasting... Okay, I have once or twice. Okay, maybe five times.
I'm just taking a little break from work. No, we have not made any gay friends. They don't exist here.
I help Ali with school. I make Jared lunch. I make dinner. I sample whatever culinary offerings they have here, which are few. But they do have one thing I love here, which is a Spudnut.
I said SPUDNUT, mom. It's like a fried donut on crack, made from potato flour. Other than that, it's Olive Gardens and Red Robins and Red Lobsters. And I even had a Hot Dog on a Stick this week, God forbid.
Look, I've got to go. Jared's awake and heading downstairs. Bye.
Love you too mom.

Looks like I missed happy hour. Or did it start early – again – today?
Piss off. I'm so bored here. What do you expect me to do?

Maybe get a job? Meet some friends? Make an effort?

At what restaurant am I going to get a job managing here? The Outback? No thanks.
And friends? Honey, I've tried. There's no one here like us. I see the way they look at me, like I'm from RuPaul's Drag Race.
God knows what Ali goes through every day. This has to be the whitest, straightest place on Earth. And everyone golfs all day. You know I fucking hate golf. And don't even get me started on Pickle Ball...

Look, our house is done soon. That should keep you busy. Pick out some drapes.
Drapes. I've picked out drapes. For fuck's sake, I'm turning into goddamned Doris Day. I drink and pick out drapes.
And shop online. That's my life here. I hate it here... enough about me. How are you doing?
Traumatized by the nuclear meltdown you witnessed yesterday?

It was not a nuclear meltdown.

Cough

An old tunnel collapsed. I feel fine. Look, we will get through this. I go back to work on Monday.
And you... you just need to make an effort. Get out, exercise... try.
Honey, I've tried. It ain't happening. Do you want me to try to make friends with the Wicked Witch across the street?
Maybe I can help her make voodoo dolls, or stir up big cauldrons of dead people soup. Maybe a Witch's Brew cooking circle. Book club?

Look honey, I know this is not Seattle. And I love you so much for going on this journey with me...
Can you quit using the word "journey"? I would not equate moving to a haunted radiated town a "journey."
Maybe a journey into the deep dark depths of hell...

When did you get so damn negative? You were never like this before.
In the two months since we got here, you've changed. You used to love exercising, and cooking, and were fun to be around. Now...

...it seems like you're just spiraling back downward into I don't know what – the days of Van and Roses again.
I don't want to be here! Ali doesn't want to be here. And living across the street from Hocus Pocus over there isn't helping. I have to see those wack-ass sticks out my kitchen window all day.
And you are not here for any of this – no, I have not changed. You've changed. You're turning into a Richland, or let's call it Witchland, Stepford Husband.
Like you couldn't care less about how your family feels, which at the moment is very shitty.

Give me a fucking break. Everything I'm doing here is for us – better job, more money, new house.
Why let some stupid sticks turn you into a lunatic who drinks all day, staring out your kitchen window. If the sticks bother you so much, go take them.
See what happens. Might give you the thrill you are obviously lacking now in your awful life.

That's exactly what I'm going going to do. Thanks for such a great idea. You are so God damn perfect.
Or, if you are so unphased by this shit show of a town, even acting so damn calm and cool after being exposed to nuclear, or plutonium, or whatever the hell kind of radiation it is, why don't you go take a God damn stick and shove it up your radiated ass.
CLINCK

You know what, I'll take that dare. But I'm going to shove it up your drunk ass.
... Jared ... I was just kiddi...

No!
No!
No!
No!
No!
No!
No!
No!
No!
What the?

You dared me – here's a whole stack of her stupid sticks. Now it's over. Let's move on.
Forget the witch. Enjoy life. Enjoy Witchland, I mean Richland.

Wait, did you see her? What's out...

Well, nothing's happened yet.
No, no sign of her. Or anyone. All good.

And no sign of The Crucible over there.
I think I'm in the clear?

So... what are we going to do with those?
I thought they were going up someone's ass.
I really don't want those anywhere near me... let's get rid of them.

No...no...no

WHIRRRRRZZZZ

Whoooossh

AAAAAAAAAAAHH

Chapter SEVEN
Week Five

Good morning – there's a coffee ready for you.
Thanks. Is Pops already gone?
Why so early?
He was supposed to return to work today – but he extended another day.
He was up all night with weird dreams – and talking – well actually kind of chanting jibberish – in his sleep. He kept me up all night too.
I think he has the flu or something. So, I'm playing the role of Nurse Ratched today.
Pops never gets sick. Are you sure it's not because of what happened last week with the tunnel? And can you please please please ease up on the wine?
I'm getting so worried about both of you that I can't focus on school. And I heard you two fighting last night. You never fought like that in Seattle. What's happening to us.

Honey, I'm fine. He'll be fine. We had an argument, no biggie. It happens.
What do you have going on today. See you after school?
Probably. Dana invited me over, but I have lots of homework. I should be around.
Okay. See you after school?
You didn't hear anything I just said. You have really got to stop staring over there. It's going to drive you mad.
I can't help it. I want to see her, just once, in the daylight.
I have to tell you... I find myself looking over at all hours... and I think she ventures out at 10:00 every night.
I'm dying to know where she goes.
Dad, don't do anything stupid!

Like I would. I'm not going near those sticks. Or that house. I'm just curious...
Dad, you said Pops is talking and chanting in his sleep. What is he saying?
I have no clue. It's in chanting. I don't think it's in English.
I need to hear what that sounds like. Can you record him chanting for me?
It might be important. I have to go to school now, but I have time to look into this later.
Please text it to me when you get it.

Uhhh...sure. Let me see what I can do.
Sniff
Sniff

Chapter EIGHT
1949 ... Meet Judith

We are so proud of you Judith, and your school accomplishments. I'm going to miss you so much.
Don't cry Mother. I'll be home in a year... just a year!
It will fly by! And when I get back, I can meet my new baby sister!
Be safe Judith. Make us proud. And remember - you are doing the Lord's work. Don't forget to write us every Sunday.
I won't forget. I'll miss you both. All three of you! I love you.
6 months later.
Judith, I hear from the Pastor that you've done well over the last few months. They are so pleased to have you there.
Tomorrow, let's do something special, as a family. Maybe a picnic. John, wouldn't that be lovely, to show Judith some of the countryside?

Yup.
Here, I made you special drink. You'll like it I think! Take a drink!

SNAP

Sanguinem
leporis cape.
Sanguinem
leporis cape.
Sanguinem
leporis cape.
Sanguinem
leporis cape.
Sanguinem
leporis cape.
Sanguinem
leporis cape.
Sanguinem
leporis cape.

Judith, dear, I need you to wake up. Judith, please wake up.
I have some awful news. We've just been sent word from America... there's been some sort of accident.
At your father's work. They need you back home. Judith, something awful has happened to your father.

Chapter NINE
Week Six

Hey you. How was school? Where've you been?
School was fine. I've been doing some research, trying to figure out what might be wrong with Pops.
I think I'm getting somewhere.

Research on what?

Oh, I forgot to tell you. Ali has a tape of your jibber jabber chanting.
She's trying to figure things out. Ali, your father seems to be getting worse.
He has had a few more seizures, or... episodes.

Why doesn't he go to the hospital?
I took him to Urgent Care today. They just think he has the flu. And is stressed. They gave him meds, thank God.

It's been a week now. The flu doesn't give you seizures. And you – are you back now to just constant drinking?
We seem to be falling apart here.
Honey, I'm just a bit under the weather...
... and going through a bit of a rough patch. And Van's fine – he's taking good care of me. Cut him a little slack. We'll be okay.
What happened at school?

Well, the word is officially out that I have two gay white dads, when I don't think this town is used to black people or gay people.
I feel like a bit of a freak here.

And it doesn't help that we are still living across the street from a witch.
Gurl, don't get me started. And those sticks...

Jesus, enough with the sticks! I'm going to bed.

The sticks totally freak me out too.
There are supposedly freaks all over town who've either knocked that stupid pile over, or, God forbid, grabbed a stick, and gone bat shit crazy.

Look, there's one of them out there now.
I can't...

Dad...what's wrong?
I'm embarrassed to tell you.
Tell me what?

We got in a fight. Me and Jared. I dared Jared to take a stick, and he did. Oh Jesus. And not just one stick.
He took them all – the whole fucking pile.
Are you guys insane? What if that's why he's so sick?
Where are the sticks now?

I threw them all out that night. They're gone. Well, they were gone, until they came flying back up through the disposal.
Christ, I'm losing my mind. Maybe you're right, this is why Jared's so sick.

I keep telling myself it's the radiation, he was exposed when the tunnel collapsed... but that can't be it.
He's having horrific nightmares, and those seizures. I don't know what to do.

This can't go on. Pops has to go to talk to his work – at least file a Worker's Comp claim or something.
This might all be because of that tunnel. We can't just ignore that – he has to let them know what is happening to him!
Honey, he's done that. They are saying it's not work-related, and has nothing to do with the tunnel collapse.

That's messed up. And you – you need to get your shit together, and put this wine away.
We can't go through this again, not like last time. Please, Dad...
...And I have an idea about those sticks. I'm going to end this. For us, and for Shannon too.

I'm going out – I need to do more research at the Library. I'm on to something.
And knowing Pops grabbed those sticks changes everything.

Sanguis in lepore ...
Sanguis in lepore ...
Sanguis in lepore ...

Jesus! What? What's going on?
I don't know. It was another dream. This one was bad. God.

We need to get you to a hospital. These dreams are going to make us both crazy.
I don't know what to do. We can't go on like this.
No hospital. I feel okay. It's the nights that are the worst.
These dreams are just so messed up. And my head hurts. Give me another day or two. Let these pills do their job.

This is too much. I'm going to lose my mind. You've already lost yours.
You need to get back to work. And have a normal night's sleep.
These dreams... is she in them? What happens in the dreams?

I don't know... it's a lot of me being chased by something... blood... screaming... just like total chaos.
And yes, she is always there. Always. Pointing at me, chanting at me, screaming at me.

I'm going over there. I want to meet her.
Please don't. Just stay away from there. We are moving into our new place any day now.

I want to talk to her. Hell, maybe I can help her.

ARRRGH!

Jared, I love you, but you have GOT to stop screaming.
I'm going to have a heart attack.
She's there - right there!

She was just right there!
No one is there. She's not here.

Can't you see her? God help me, why can't you leave me ALONE!
That's it, I'm going over there now.

Ahhh!

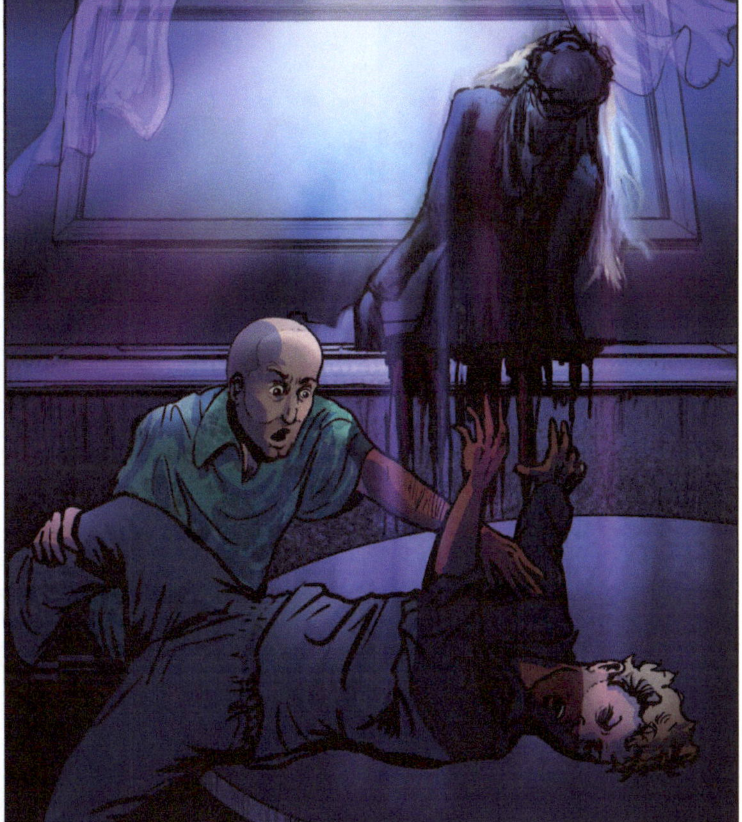

It's just us honey. Just us. Calm down.
I'm okay... I'm okay now.

Good. I'm going over there now.
Please don't leave me. I'm really scared.

Van, she's here - she's right there! You can't tell me you don't see her!
Honey, no one is here. You're hallucinating.

Is she gone? Do you still see her?

I think she's gone.
I'm going now. It's not 10 yet – she should still be there.
You're okay. Just stay here, in bed. Will you be okay for a few minutes?

I'm okay now. I'm awake, it's over. But I don't want you to go...
...I'll be right back. This ends tonight.

RRRING

Knock
Knock
Knock

Eeek!

You scared the shit out of me.
Give me a sec.

Hi. I take it you are the woman who lives here. I'm Van. Yes, Van, like you know, a big boxy car.
I live across the street. My husband Jared and our daughter Ali moved in a few months ago. We haven't met. I just wanted to... make an introduction...
...sorry I didn't like bring a cake, or a casserole or anything... and, say that if you ever need anything, now you know who we are.

And while we're chatting... I have to apologize for something.
We were drinking wine, sometimes I drink too much but I'm not really adjusting to this town very well, so I tend to go a bit overboard with the chardonnay, but I'm working on that. Anyway, we got in a fight.
And I dared my husband – yes, I have a husband, and yes, we have a Black daughter who you've probably seen around
– and yes, dares are still a thang, even in your fabulous forties – okay, fifties – anyways, I dared him to come grab one of these cute sticks.
You know, just to see what it was, since they are like always out here. I didn't think he'd do it, but...

GO!

Ummm, go? Okay, but since he took a stick – actually, again, not sure why, but he took the whole pile –
he's been feeling a bit sick and out of sorts... and has had several nights of bad dreams...

HA ha ha ha ha

I know, right? Anyhoo, does this have anything to do with your stick? Sticks.
Can you recommend a remedy?
Can we replace them for you? Anything to make this better would be like really great.

Sanguinem leporis cape!

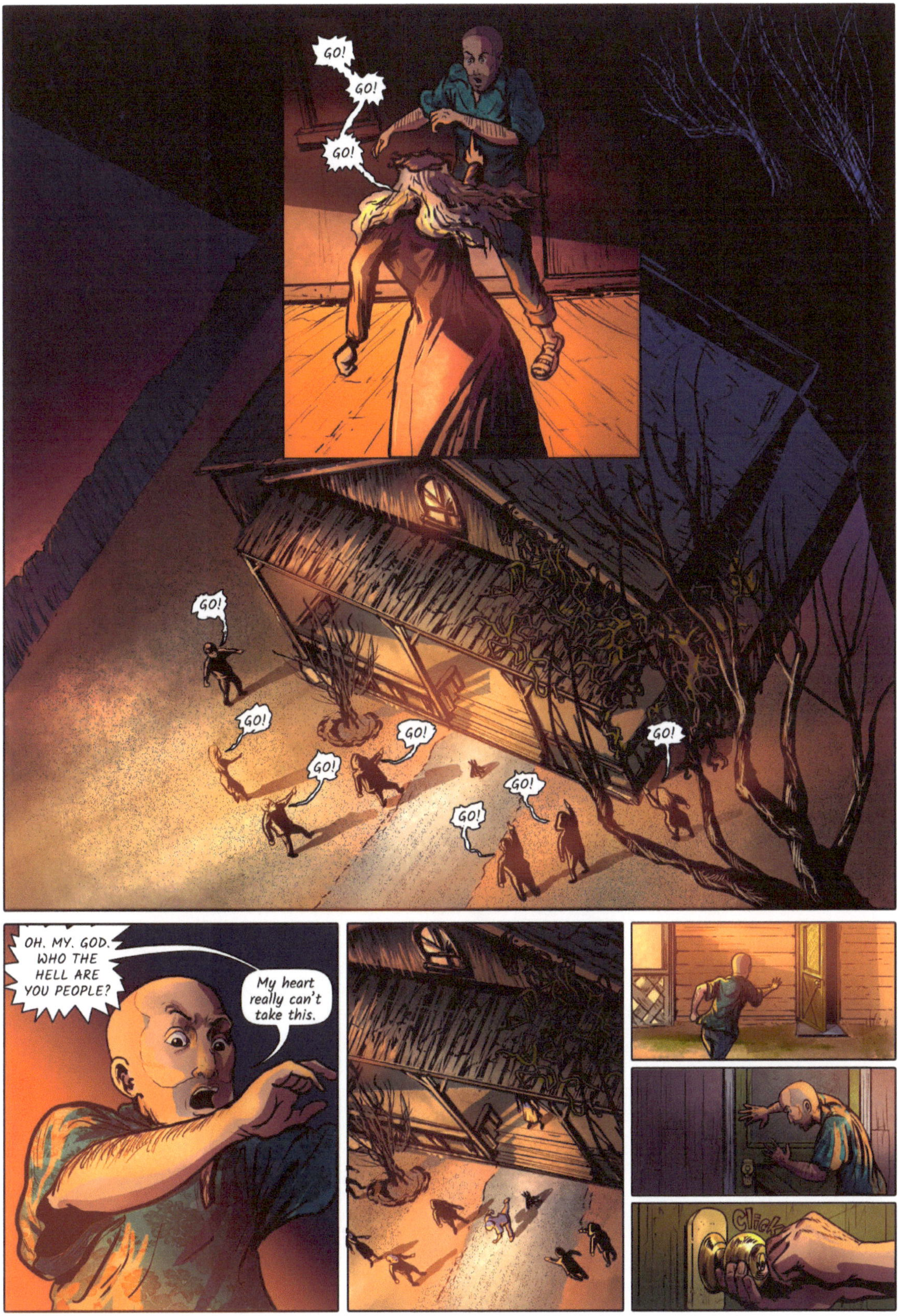

GO!
GO!
GO!
GO!
GO!
GO!
GO!
GO!
GO!
GO!

Chapter TEN
Week Six - The next day

Thanks so much for coming over Brett. I really need someone to talk to about all of this, and didn't really know who else to call.
I don't really have any close friends here. So thanks...

It's okay. Just kind of weird. I was surprised to get your call. Not sure how I can help with anything. And I have to admit I'm not really comfortable being here, being so close to
–you know– that house over there.

Hey, is it true you have two gay dads?
Oh, yes, that is true. Yes, I have two awesome dads. No biggie. One of them's upstairs now.

Have you seriously never been around a gay person? That's so messed up.
Calm down.
That's not why I called you here. I actually asked you here for a different reason.

It's about her.
Her? Who her?

Her. The witch.
What about her?

The sticks. My stupid drama queen dads got in like a drunk fight and one of my dads dared the other to go grab one of those sticks.
And he did. And not just one. He took them all.

Oh shit. This is bad.
This is really fucking bad. I don't think I should be here. I've got to go.

Wait. Please help me. I know you were there when Shannon did the same thing. Shannon told me about it. And look at her now – she's not okay. She's a mess. She has nightmares, she wanders around whispering and talking to herself.
She cries and laughs at nothing, sometimes right in front of the Witch's house. Look, I know you guys dated for years. Don't you want to help her. You put her up to it!

I hate to even think about that night. It was the worst night of my life. Yes, I dared Shannon to tip the sticks over. But she – she freaked out, and kicked them, then went up to the door, then actually reached down and took that stupid stick.
And she – the Witch – she was there at the door, pointing at Shannon. I can't get that image out of my head as hard as I try.

And now my dad is upstairs sick in bed. He too is having those same nightmares.
Part of me thinks it's maybe like, the nuclear reactors or something where he works. He was there when that tunnel collapsed last week. But the doctors are saying that's not it. And now I know he also took that whole pile of witch sticks.

You're right – since then, Shannon too is different. Beyond different. I don't even recognize her anymore, she's gotten so weird.
And she's always talking about demons, and her...

That's why I broke up with her. I want to help her, but I can't deal with it anymore.
Then help me. Let's make this right. I have a plan. But I need your help.

What kind of help?
Look, I've been doing a bunch of research.
About witchcraft, sticks, curses, rituals. And chanting, especially the chanting. I have looked up everything you just described with Shannon – nightmares, animal blood, freaky masks, you name it.
And I found something, something that matches this chanting.

What? What are you talking about? How do you know it matches the chanting?
I taped my dad's nightmares, and his chanting. I'm telling you, I know what to do. But... we need her to be there also.

Wait, not her – the Witch? No fucking way Ali. I don't want anything to do with it, or her. You should drop this. You're playing with fire.

There's no way we can drop this – it's too late for that. Look, I learned about Judith. Yes, her dad died at Hanford when she was away. But her mom did not die of cancer – she died in childbirth.
Her baby died also – Judith's sister – she was born deformed – like many other babies born in Richland during that time.

I think that's where she goes every night – to mourn her dead baby sister.
Richland, and Hanford, have ruined her life completely. And she's pissed.

Wait. Are you saying she goes to the Dead Baby Cemetery at night?

God is that what it's called? Where is it?
It's just outside of town, in the woods. It's full of Downwinder babies buried there, who died in the 50's.
They say that if you go there at night, you can hear babies crying for their mothers. That place is haunted...

Yes, it is haunted! By her. She's haunting it. That's where she goes. We have to go there. I need to take my Pops there, and you need to get Shannon there. Can you do that?

There's no way in hell I'm going to the Dead Baby Cemetery. No way. Yes, this whole town is scary – but that's beyond. No way.

How can you be so sure this would work anyways?

Look... I think I found a way to fix this. For my Pops, for Shannon – and you and I can make this happen.
Brett, you put her up to this – help me make things right! Or we can do nothing, and Shannon and my dad just end up like all of the other crazy people walking around this town. I see them almost every day, staring at the Witch's house.

Hey Pops, how're you doing?

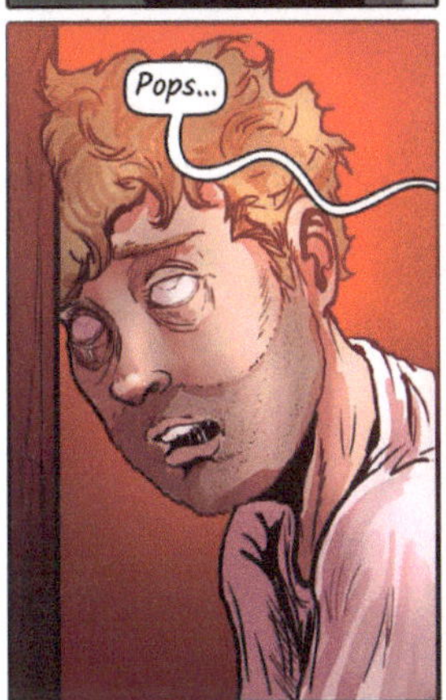
Pops...

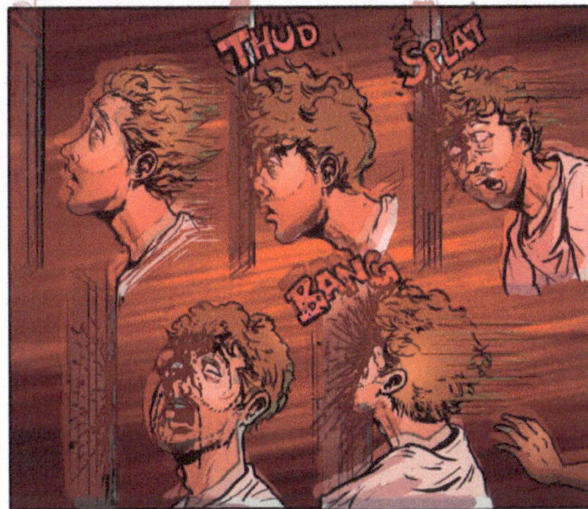
THUD
SPLAT
BANG

Pops! Stop! Oh my God, what are you doing?

Virgulae ... Maledictio ... Virgulae ... Maledictio...
Jesus, dude... Ali, what's happening?

Pop, it's okay. You're sleepwalking.
I'm here, everything is okay.

Pop, it's okay... you're sleepwalking... I'm here... everything is okay.

No No No No No...

THUD
THUD THUD

Pops, stop! Stop!

Hey kids, wassup?

Sweet Jesus, what is happening here? Is everyone okay? You all look like you've just seen a ghost... or a witch... What's going on?
Pops just had an episode. He was hitting his head against the wall, and thought he saw the Witch, who's obviously not here. Can you help get him upstairs, and get him cleaned up?

Oh my God, Jared. Jared, honey, let's go get you cleaned up.

Cough
Cough

Brett... now you know what is happening here.
Jesus...

Okay then. Tonight. It has to be tonight. It's Saturday. It's the only night that we can really pull this off. Please?
Let's meet out there at 9:45. I'll bring my dads. Just show up with Shannon.
And... I know this is an odd request... is there any way you can bring... a dead animal? Maybe roadkill? I beg you...

Roadkill?
Brett please, it's important.

Okay, okay, I'll do it. I'll bring Shannon tonight to the Dead Baby Cemetery.
Oh, and yes, I will look for a dead animal to bring along as well. Good times.

And... can we go there now? I want to scope it out in advance, and find her baby sister's grave.
Jesus. Roadkill. What the fuck?

Chapter ELEVEN
Week Six - Later that day

This is crazy. The first time out of the house in a week and this is where you are taking your sick father?
Where the hell are we? And you know my head has been throbbing again, all day today. This isn't really helping.
Just trust me. I know this seems messed up. Look at it as a family adventure.
I thought you said we were going to get ice cream, for Shannon's birthday. I take it that is not happening. What is this place?

Oh Jesus, a cemetery? Ali, what the fuck is happening? Can't we have a normal night where we go to a Baskin Robbins like a normal American family?
Really Ali, please just be honest with us – what's actually happening here?

I'm sorry. I lied about the ice cream. And it's not Shannon's birthday. But please, I need you to trust me on this. Think of this as a family journey, using your favorite phrase. We're trail blazing.

In a cemetery?

Yes, Pops. I have a plan to get you well.

Jesus Christ. Well great, I just pissed myself.
Oh, hi Brett. We keep meeting in the oddest circumstances. Ali, explain to us what we are doing here.

Brett, I don't want to be here. I should not be here.
And she would definitely not like me to be here.
She? Your mom?

Judith.
This is not right. Brett, why are we here? What's happening? Ali? What's going on? She's really not going to like this.

Okay, I need everyone to calm down. Brett and I brought you here to help you. Yes, this is a cemetery –
This is the Dead Baby Cemetery. It's where all of the babies that died from radiation in the early days of Hanford are buried.
Another Witchland hotspot.

Pops, please, just roll with it. Have I ever steered you wrong? I'm going to try to help you. What happened to you also happened to Shannon... and I am going to do my best to rid both of you of the Witch's spell.
Just do it for me, please? Now... I need everyone to just sit here, behind these trees, quietly.

It's almost time. I'll be right back.

All I know is that what has happened to you Pops, and you Shannon, and probably many others over the past 50 years, is some bad juju.

Based on the chanting, the dreams you guys are having, and the sticks, I believe this to be the result of a curse, and after much research into dark spells, I think this is the only cure.

Wah Wah Wah Wah Wah

Oh Jesus was that a baby ghost? Really Ali?
SHHH... she'll be here soon. No one make a sound.

Wah Wah Wah

Soror mea infantula.
Soror mea infantula.

Judith, I know something bad happened to you when you went away.
It's not your fault what they did to you. And what happened to your dad, all those years ago at Hanford. And your mom. And...

... to her.
To all these poor babies. I know you are hurting. But I think I can help you also.

Okay, now. I know this is scary, and messed up. But all of you come over here now.
She can't hurt us while she's in the circle. But we don't have long... it wears off.

We have to go fast. Pops, Shannon, I need you both to drop to your knees, right here.

You!
You!
Oh hi... neighbor. Yes, it's me. I'm sorry it's come to this, and that we've had to trap you in some sort of salt circle?
I tried to work it out with you on your terms, but you wouldn't listen.

Wait, what? You've met before?
And spoken with her? In person? When?
I wouldn't say I spoke WITH her. I tried.
I went over there yesterday when you were gone – I apologized, and I have to admit I rambled on a bit – but I asked for help. She screamed at me, and then spoke in tongues.
I've been a wreck ever since, and my head has not stopped pounding.

Dude, you'd better get on your knees also.

Come join me down here, honey... let's do this together.

Now, take out your hands.

Ow! Damn gurl! That hurt!

Brett... the bag.
Oh shit. Okay. Here goes.

Now, each of you squeeze a few drops of blood onto this...
what is that?
That better not be a dead pet.
It's a dead rat. My grandpa keeps traps in his yard.
thump

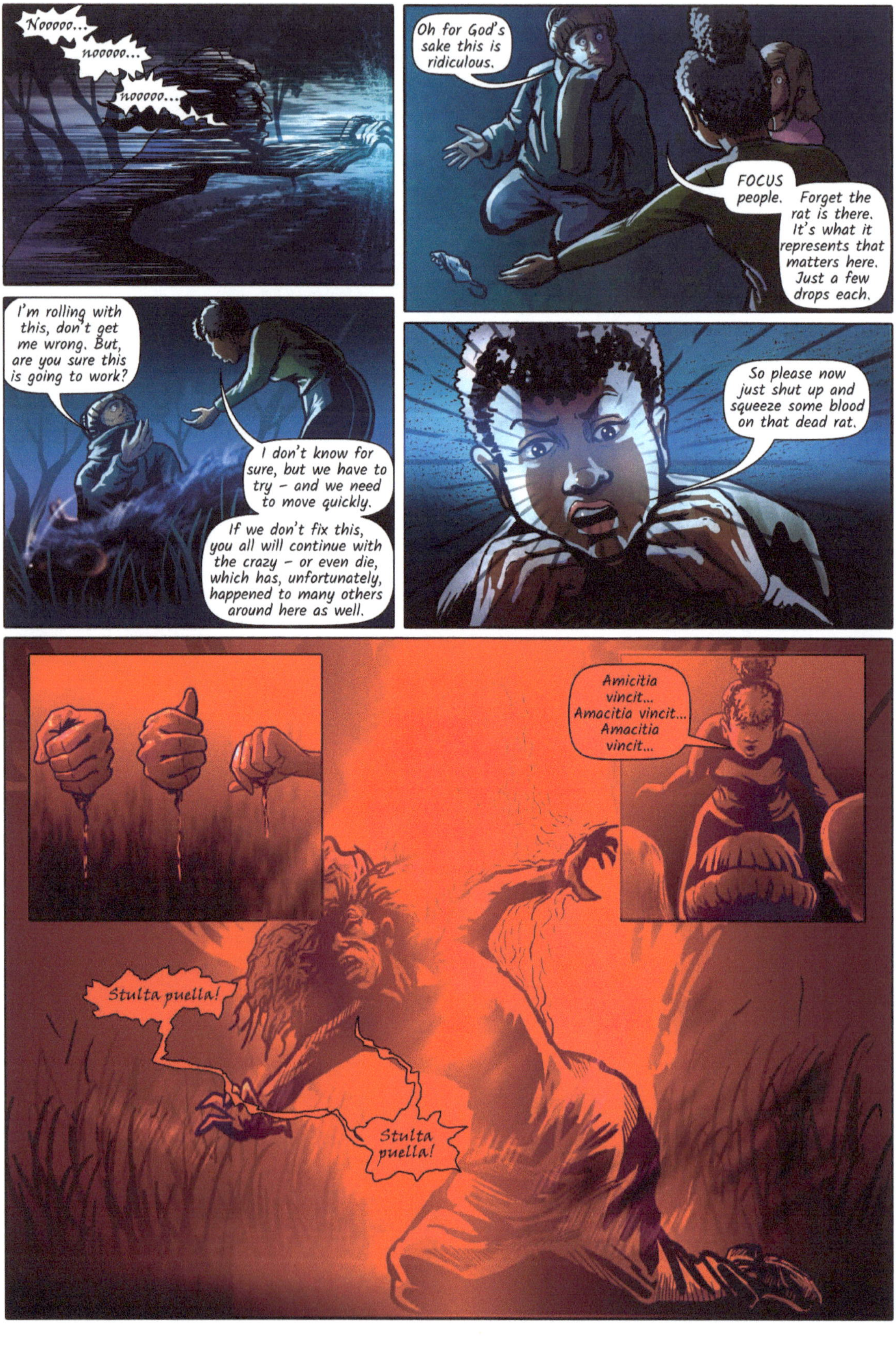

Amicitia vincit... Amacitia vincit... Amacitia vincit...

Stulta puella!

Stulta puella!

Amcitia vincit...
Amcitia vincit...
Amcitia vincit...

VASE RETRO STRIX NUMQUAM SUADE MIHI VANA! SUNT MALA QUAE LIBAS! IPSE VENENA BIBAS!

Did it work?

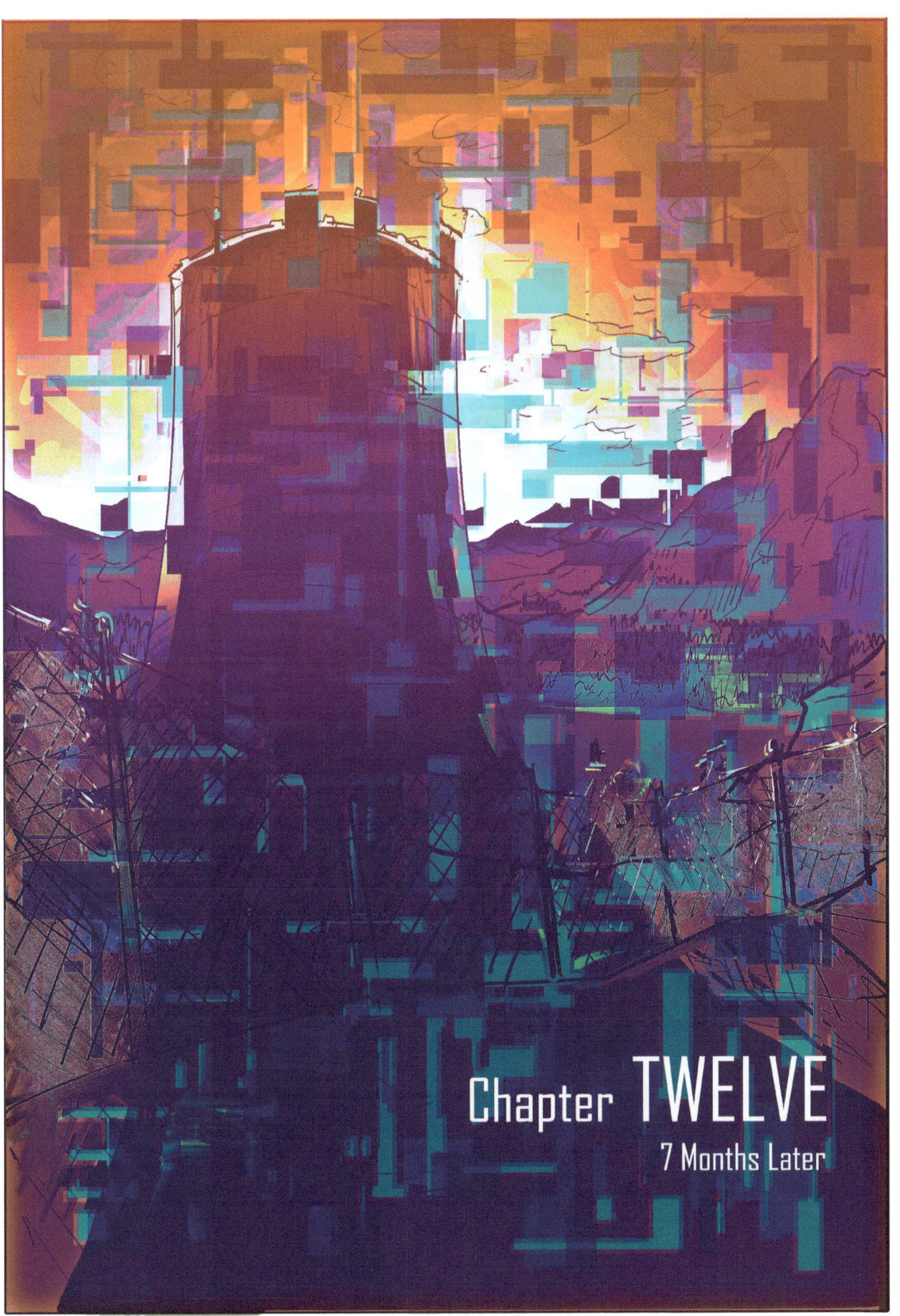
Chapter TWELVE
7 Months Later

Their New Place...

Thank you all for coming tonight, and celebrating our beautiful Valedictorian daughter Ali, Brett and Shannon on your big accomplishment
– graduation from Richland High School!

Go Bombers!

Hear Hear! To your delicious Chicken Divan...
and also to my amazing Dad's seven months of sobriety!

Now, I wish I had something real in these glasses to serve you, but we don't allow that in the house anymore.
So sorry. But hopefully you all enjoyed my specialty – and namesake – Chicken DiVAN.

Van, Jared, your new house is so great.
Thanks for having us over – but also thanks in advance for the entire summer ahead of us, full of water skiing and boating.
And letting me be the Captain of that sweet boat. I'm so stoked.

Uh, that would be a no. Shannon, it's our pleasure – it's been such a godsend having you in Ali's life, and our life, over the past year.
And I'm glad you and Brett are back together... We are so proud of your success, and the fact that all three of you are heading off to college.

Guess what's for dessert...
spudnuts!

Probably the greatest thing to happen to us this crazy year is my darling Dad becoming the manager of Richland's very own culinary landmark, the Spudnut Shack.
And we've all gained many many pounds because of it.

Honey, don't get me started. I'm trying to wean myself of of those damn spudnuts... but they've become my vice since going on the wagon.
How's the clean up project going Jared? I'll likely be seeing you around this summer - I start my internship out there next week.
I'll be working out there as well - I'll probably see you around.

It's going well.
COUGH
COUGH
COUGH
Probably another year on this one project, then we'll see after that.

Hey kids, not to bring us back to the dark times, but I do hear all the latest Witchland gossip at the restaurant. And word on the street is that Miss Judith has been... institutionalized.
She is no longer living in that house, and now is the newest resident to that new Nursing Home out in Kennewick.

Cough
Cough
Maybe now she'll get the mental help she probably has needed for decades.

Judith's New Home

Well hello there... and who do we have here?
Welcome to your new home...

...Judith! Miss Judith, we are happy to have you join us. We promise to take good care of you.
If you need anything, just holler or press the nurse call button. I'll be back in a while with your dinner.

What the?
Klack

HHAAAA
HAHAHA
HEHEEE
HAHAHA

Cough
Cough
Cough

COUGH

COUGH

The hell...

Attention Hanford employees. This is an emergency update. There has been a biohazard breach. I repeat, there has been a biohazard breach. All employees, please take cover.
Remain in your offices until further notice. I repeat, there has been a breach in biohazard security. Please take cover until further notice.

www.ingramcontent.com/pod-product-compliance
Lightning Source LLC
Chambersburg PA
CBHW040823050726
47507CB00021B/117

9798987920398